THE EDGE

DAWN

LOCKDOWN ANTHOLOGY

Stephen M Taylor

Copyright © 2021

Stephen Mark Taylor

All rights reserved

The characters and events portrayed in this book are fictitious. Any similarity to real persons, living or dead is coincidental and not intended by the Author.

No part of this book may be reproduced, stored in a retrieval system, transmitted in any form or by any means, electronic, mechanical, photocopying, recording or otherwise, without express written permission of the publisher.

Second Edition

ISBN - 9798506696971

For Louise. You read my stories in the early days and always gave your honest appraisal.

Forever in my thoughts.

INTRODUCTION

Covid-19 has affected each one of us – the world over. Lockdown was especially hard, with the lack of travel, holidays, eating out and a hundred other things that we were unable to do.

Writing is always an escape and a place where you can create and be someone else. This collection of short stories, written throughout the lockdown's of 2020 and 2021, gave a welcome, if only brief, respite from the four walls.

I hope you enjoy reading them – I certainly enjoyed writing them.

Stephen M Taylor.

CONTENTS

1. Grandad's Cabin
2. The Girl Under The Stairs
3. Jack
4. The Voice In The Room
5. What Happened Last Night
6. Waiting For The Number Thirty-Six Bus
7. Face Masks At A Funeral
8. The Test
9. Sweet Dreams
10. Twenty-Six Primrose Street
11. A Story By The Campfire

GRANDAD'S CABIN

The sky, overcast and grey, looked ominous as the clouds thick with the impending rain floated slowly across the lake towards the cabin – which stood like a beacon against the green canvas of the forest. It had stayed dry for the three days he had been here, not a single drop had fallen, although it had been cold. Jack had checked the temperature on the little thermometer, nailed on the inside of the cabin's only door – it had read -2 degrees Celsius. Cold enough to freeze the balls off a brass monkey, his Grandad used to say, when the winter chill came blowing in from the North.

Back when he was a child, his Grandad would bring him up here fishing and trapping. They would pull out salmon from the river beyond the lake, decent sized ones too, and catch themselves a few rabbits or pheasant even. Jack loved his time here with his Grandad, the open air and the peaceful stillness that you would only find deep in the wilds - a place he would often visit in his dreams. When things started to turn bad. Today he would hunt. The mouldy tins, he had eaten - along with the meagre rations he had brought along – hunger now settled its icy spike inside his guts, it needed slaking.

With the weather looking grim, Jack would need to move fast. One thing to avoid, at all costs, was being outdoors when the storms hit. He glanced at the small table in the cabin's single room living area, and spotted the knife, along with a few other items he had discarded on there when he had first arrived. His mobile phone bleeped weakly at him – informing Jack that it would be soon out of battery – not that it mattered. The nearest phone signal was at least twenty miles away and internet access was as futuristic and marvellous – and as likely – as a spaceship landing outside, full of advanced, intelligent alien life.

That was all part of the charm, no contact with the outside world, no one knowing he was here, just he alone with nature, living the life he always dreamt of. His only neighbours were a family of blue tits in the tree outside, and occasional visitors to the yard – foxes and red squirrels mostly.

Jack pulled on the large waxy jacket, his gloves and the woolly hat that he had left by the door. The rifle was standing on its butt end, leant against the wall and he scooped it up on the way out.

Stepping outside, the chill wind blowing in across the lake hit him like a hammer, taking his breath for a few seconds. It was cold – he would need to be quick. The ground was hard under his feet still but in a few hours it would quickly turn to mud and walking would be difficult; he had seen it so many times. It comes without warning up here.

Jack had walked a hundred yards into the forest before he heard the familiar noises of his quarry, the shuffling and scurrying in the undergrowth. He paused, leaning against a tree to cock the gun, feeling the click as it engaged and he once again felt the rush of the impending kill. The paused turned into a wait – patience was always the word (according to Grandad). Ten minutes passed, still Jack waited. Then, sniffing the air for danger out popped a rabbit. Jack was down wind so his scent carried away on the breeze, and did not alert the creature. It took a few more steps into the open and began nibbling at the grass.

It was a quick kill, the bullet taking the rabbit just behind the ears and snuffing out its life without it even realising. Jack trotted over and picked up the carcass, throwing it over his shoulder and heading back to the cabin.

The smell as it cooked was delicious, Jack's stomach growled appreciatively. The cabin had an open fire, over which the rabbit was rotating on a small spit. Its fat and juices dripped down into the pan that was set underneath. He would use it as a spread later, once it had cooled.

Jack thought that he had never tasted anything as delicious in all his life, ripping the meat from the bone ravenously, the juice running down his chin. A smile touched his lips, a smile often perceived as cold and unfeeling.

His thoughts turned to the reason he was here at all, twenty years after his last visit. Hands rubbed together involuntary and he could feel the blisters on his thumbs and palms sore and open. The work carried out to receive those blisters had been necessary. He pictured his first day here, cold, tired but with a purpose – one that had driven him to lock up the house, leaving everything behind and drive the three hundred miles out into the forest to the cabin.

There was no other choice; the alternative had no appeal whatsoever. Jack's wife, Marie, had said as much. Her incessant whining and moaning drove him crazy at times – but he had learned to live with it, to switch off and drift away into a faraway state – one in which his mind seemed to belong to someone else, someone who was in control.

The rain started to fall. Light at first but then large, penny-sized droplets bouncing off the roof of the cabin, making it sound like he was on the inside of a very large steel drum. The noise was deafening, but comforting at the same time. It instantly transported him back to when he was six, lain awake listening to the rage of the storm outside. Rain, sleet and wind, all combining to create one humdinger of a North Eastern. Jack remembered the feeling of awe and of being a little afraid, scared that the cabin was going to be ripped out of the ground, and carried away into the air, away to who knew where. Lost forever.

That never happened, of course, but sometimes the feelings of youth stay with us, surfacing in times of stress to remind us of what could be, of what might happen to us if we don't conform.

Marie wanted to argue, he could feel it. Deep down, he knew it would come to this, eventually. There were tears on her part, which usually happened, but this time, it grated him – rubbed him up the wrong way. The eyes glistened, the lower lip came out and Jack knew she was over the edge. Still, he baited and provoked. She threw the letter at him; it hit him in the chest and fell limply to the floor. He stared at it for a long time, before bending to retrieve it. The contents were not a shock, although it knocked the breath from him nonetheless. Four words stood out starkly on the cream coloured sheet of paper, with the official looking letterhead at the top. Those words were 'Notice of Divorce Proceedings'.

Jack had refused, shaking his head slowly and staring blankly into space as the gravity of it crashed home. "No," he said. "It's not happening," he added after.

She had screamed at him then – into his face, telling him all the things he did not want to hear. Truth has a funny way of finding the hidden places in the psyche, and going to town on them, tugging and pulling, accusing, berating. This is what happened; this is how she caused him to snap. The threat of "I am taking Anna and I am going - we are leaving and you won't see her or me again," sealed the deal.

Jack could just not let that happen. The red mist descended – so they say – although he had never really understood that statement until that moment. He did actually see red, and something inside of him snapped.

The rain continued to fall outside, heavier now and more persistent. Suddenly, he needed to be out in the cool evening air, breathing in the crispness – the beauty of it. The rain was bitterly cold on his exposed skin – his jacket still hung on the peg inside the door. Jack found himself by the stand of trees to the right of the cabin – halfway between *it* and the lake shoreline. The cover from the trees relieved the cold somewhat – although Jack barely noticed.

Marie was the reason he was here. She wanted to take his daughter away from him, forever. What kind of mother does that to a kid? Denying the father his right to spend time with his child was wrong. How would she have liked it?

Jack squatted by the small mound of freshly dug earth, gazing at the footprints that surrounded it. He would have to do something about that – after all – it made the place look untidy. If he were planning to spend some serious time up here then it would need putting right. For now though, it would keep.

He walked back over to the cabin, pausing for a moment before opening the boot of the car. The smell hit him, making his eyes water and gag involuntary. Marie stared back at him, her face (or what was left of it) a rictus of horror, still covered in dried blood along the edges of the cut made by the axe – which incidentally – was still embedded deep into her skull.

Anna was his first priority, he wanted to make sure she was comfortable and at rest – her passing had been less messy, just a pillow and a bit of force.

Marie on the other hand. Well, she had struggled and so it became an ordeal – not just for her but Jack too. He would deal with her tomorrow. Maybe.

He was hungry again, the grumble deep down in his guts told him as much. He was absently rubbing at the blisters on his hand again, causing one to pop open and dribble pus across his fingers. He took one last look at his wife, her eyes still wide open – accusing him - before slamming the boot shut, sealing her in.

The rest of the rabbit went down a treat. He cleaned up the few dishes in the sink, with water from the lake, and then settled down for the night. He would need rest, tomorrow promised to be a busy day.

THE GIRL UNDER THE STAIRS

She had been there for as long as I could remember. Her hair golden, and a mousy little face, always around always in the background looking in - never really part of things but there nonetheless. Her name had been Gretchen, I think. That is what I called her but I guess I never really knew if that was her real name.

I have tried to pinpoint the exact time, or rather, how old I was when I first saw her, or the first recollection – but it evades me. It is as if a veil has gone up, blocking out everything from that time – all the feelings, the emotions and the memory.

We had a small cupboard under the stairs, one where things like the vacuum cleaner, tools and old bits of furniture are stored. At the back though, was Gretchen. Always dressed the same way – a white gown that billowed out from her ankles, white socks with a frill around the edge, and black sandal-type shoes. She would have her hair done up in pigtails, which always seemed to be just on the edge of falling apart, but never did.

She spoke sometimes, mostly in a whisper – as if it was our little secret. I would take her food and a glass of milk. She asked for cookies, but they always sat on the plate – uneaten – when I returned, as was the milk. I would take these away, throwing the biscuits in the bin and pouring the milk down the sink, making sure my parents did not spot me. As long as she asked, I would keep on bringing them to her.

Gretchen did not age. As I grew from a young boy, into a teenager, she remained the same. This never occurred to me as being odd – it was just how it was, how Gretchen was. We would sometimes play hide and seek throughout the house when Mum was out and Dad was working in the garage. However hard I tried, she always found me within minutes – whereas I spent hours looking, only to find her back in the cupboard under the stairs – which is the first place I would look – it would make me so mad!

As time wore on, and I became a man, other things became important to me. I would go out more with friends – the few I had – and involve myself more in sporting activities (I was quite good at basketball and played for the school and district teams). Gretchen started to fall further and further to the back of my mind – back into the dark recesses, amid the cobwebs and fog.

Thinking back, once I had hit sixteen, I cannot remember seeing much of her at all – even when the house was silent and empty, with just me in it. She hardly came to me, or called to me – she just 'faded away'.

It is strange really, in so many ways. Throughout my early childhood, she was a huge part of my life, sharing many things and always being there if I was upset or feeling down. I knew I had her as a go-to if I needed. Then, it just was not the same anymore and life moved on.

We had the cupboard cleared out one year and I recall being scared that she would be found and get into real trouble. Dad carried on slinging things out into the living room – no mention of her, no sign of her. I did think that she was hiding out in another room until he had finished, before taking up her place once more, but after checking later – I found the cupboard completely bare of anything.

Dad spent the next three weeks adding shelves and racking to the cupboard, so he could store his work tools away neatly. Once done, he proudly showed it to Mum and I. Gretchen was gone, and in fact, there would be no room for her if she did return, the shelves took up lots of space.

She did return though. Back into the cupboard under the stairs, making herself a little place to lay and sleep – squeezing underneath the bottom-most shelf and curling up into a ball – like a foetal baby in the womb.

One day, around the time I left school, so must be just before my seventeenth birthday, she was gone. I never saw her again. It is difficult to describe how I felt, maybe it was a feeling of loss, and maybe it was relief? Even now, I will sit and think of her, sitting cross-legged in the cupboard, her radiant smile and the raggedy pigtails threatening to fall out of place. Some people experience 'imaginary friends' as they work their way through the tricky minefield of childhood, into adolescence, but few –

if any – carry those memories into adulthood and recall them in any great detail.

I think about her often, usually when I am a little stressed or alone with my thoughts. Just lately, I feel like she is near, watching and waiting until I need her. I will walk into a room and see peripheral movement, or slight noises. A prickle of something down my spine, as if an ice cube is slowly making its way down my back – leaving a chilly trail as it goes.

The house was an old one, at least a few hundred years I think – although I have never really checked to find out exactly. What I have done though, is research a few articles at the library – spending long afternoons under the buzz of the overhead fluorescents, set high into the ceiling above, sending down their glare so I could read. One book in particular caught my eye; it was a thick, red hardback titled 'tales of mystery'. It was by an Author named Thomas Beck and told of a number of stories of lost children, murders and kidnappings. The thing is - Thomas Beck was my Grandfather.

The book contained lots of text and the odd picture here and there, detailing various mysteries and disappearances in the local area. It was interesting flicking through the pages, some bringing a smile to my face with their familiarity and absurdness. Then, I turned to page 127, and I froze. Gretchen stared back at me from the page, her smile radiant, and her white gown billowing and blowing in an apparent breeze. Her eyes stared from the page and right into the depths of my soul.

Gretchen was eight years old when she was reported missing. No sign or trace of her since she disappeared on September 15th 1908. She was my Grandfather's sister.

My heart was pounding against my ribcage; I could hear it as well as feel it. To me, it sounded like an Amazonian tribesman banging loudly on an animal-skin drum.

How could this be? How could I be staring at a grainy, black and white picture of a lost child from a hundred years before, one that I had seen on many occasions whilst growing up?

I could feel a headache lurking ominously behind my eyes, and I rubbed furiously at my temples, trying to release the tension and the pressure.

That is when I looked up from the book - Gretchen stood watching me. She smiled warmly – one that I had seen a thousand times before, a thousand or more years ago. She held her hand out to me, small and delicate – palms-up. A tear, so tiny I almost missed it, pooled at the corner of her left eye, before rolling down her cheek and falling from her chin to the floor.

I took her hand in mine; her skin felt cool to the touch but sparked off a million memories in my mind. The overriding thought I had at that moment was to protect. My whole life seemed to have been building up to one particular moment – one turn in the road, one hill that needed climbing. It was here. I stood, smiled, and walked out with her hand in hand, into the bright late morning sunshine of another late summer's day. It was September 15th 2008.

JACK

You just never know what you will get in this City – one day it is the best place on earth, bustling, vibrant and full of colour – the next, it feels drab and dreary; drizzle falling and dark clouds filling the grey sky.

I wander aimlessly through the streets, gazing into the shop fronts that I pass, longing to push open the door and walk in, to browse through the many wondrous things on show. How good would a new suit look on me? New shoes, shiny enough to see my face in them – Italian leather, definitely Italian leather.

A taxi shoots past, splashing up water from a puddle at the side of the road and hitting my legs. 'Thanks,' I mutter under my breath – cursing the wretched luck that I just cannot seem to shake. My jeans turn a dark shade of blue where the water saturated them, making it look like I had wet myself – not that anyone would notice.

People walk by without so much as a glance, oblivious and preoccupied with their own thoughts and problems, rushing to get to point B, from wherever their particular point A was.

A woman in a bright red raincoat and knee-length boots hurries by, giving me a slight nudge out of the way, as she goes, causing me to bump against the window of a large department store. The mannequins stare at me impassively, as if bored of standing for weeks on end, gazing out at the passing world; the clothes changed every few days their only cause of excitement.

The woman is gone in the blink of an eye, I don't even have time to shout abuse at her, or to do what I have done so many time before, so I take it out on the reflection in the plate glass window instead. It is one of an old man, haggard beyond belief, with a curly mop of greasy dark hair that shows no sign of wanting to turn grey. A rough beard covered most of the face – which was straggly and dirty looking. The clothes were ones salvaged from dustbins and skips, even a washing line.

A sorry sight if ever there was one.

The rain begins to fall again. Drizzle, turning to a more persistent rain, the drops getting large enough to bounce off the pavement as they hit with a 'splat'. All around, people run for cover – in either the shops or bus shelters. I simply carry on ambling along, allowing the rain to soak me through, to cleanse my spirit. Lifting my face to the sky, it feels liberating – standing alone on the pavement, the water running in rivulets from my hair, face and neck and down the back of my shirt, tickling the cool, exposed skin there.

How long have I wandered these very streets? Years? Centuries? Maybe millennia? There was a time whereby a man could walk out across the road and only encounter a horse and cart trundling down the rutted track that was now concrete and asphalt. Those days are gone – lost in the ethos of time and resigned to history like everything else. Time swallows up the largest of structures, down to the tiniest of molecules – nothing escapes its wrath.

I am a faceless man, a voiceless man. People don't see or hear me – instead they pass me by, flinching or shuddering slightly as they go, as if a goose walking over their grave.

On and on I walk, the weight of the world, hanging heavy – trying to squash and crush my soul. On days like today, drab and miserable, my mood often reflects it. I long and yearn for the sun to come out and brighten the City, to penetrate the gloominess and bring hope – banishing the darkness and all the creatures that lurk there. It does not last long though. For I am one of those creatures.

Today, I wear clothes from the 21st century – easily accessible and lightweight. Yesterday -or was it a hundred years ago – I wore a dark suit. Before that, a robe, tied at the waist with rope. Years and years of costume changes, of landscape changes. Many more to come no doubt once I am gone. One thing that remains constant is the people. Always the same, always in a rush, never time to stop and ponder.

The ground underneath my feet may have altered, but to me it is all the same. The tight alleyways, twisting and turning into a maze that could snare the unsuspecting traveller – which would always remain so. The dark of night caressing each stone and cobble, brick and tile, with its wicked fingers of death, sliding unseen around every corner, across every highway.

My name is Jack. That is not the name given to me at birth – that of which I simply cannot recall. The newspapers gave me the title of Jack. I quite liked it then, and I still do today. It suits me I think.

The world is a fast place now, one that I cannot seem to keep up with or comprehend. I feel as if my time may finally be reaching its conclusion – the zenith of my being. More and more these last few years (centuries), I have been found wanting – no longer able to do the things I once could. The time is drawing in fast – and my wretched body is breaking.

Old London Town - streets paved with gold. Countless souls have come to seek out fortune and fame, only to find their end – much as my own end is fast approaching. There are more like me – of that I am certain – spread across the globe like prophets of doom, dishing out fear, terror, pain – always looking out for the weak and the infirm.

I reach the end of the road – both actually and metaphorically – stepping around a group of young women and shuffling ever closer to my destination. I can see it between buildings, a murky brown reflecting what little sunlight there is and making it seem as though a million tiny lights danced just beneath the surface of this great river.

It is now my time to leave this place, the place that I have called home for so long. I shall miss it, as it shall miss me. We are both well versed in the art of killing, so in tune that we each know of one another's intricacies. The river calls to me, small waves lapping the mud banks that run the length of this serpent that dissects the streets. It is time to end this, to go home after so long, so much time.

The mud closes around my ankles and takes me in its death grip, sucking and pulling. My arms stretch out wide, like a dark angel – the dark angel that I am. I take one last look at the City, at my City, thinking one final time of all the misery I have brought to its history, all the blood let to flow along the cobbles and down into the drains – finally reaching the river. The mysteries of who I am, who I was, will stay forever within me, within the soul of London itself, in its folklore. Hundreds upon hundreds of books written and read, pored over, and yet, I remain undetected.

The mud is now above my knees, the water lapping and sloshing around. It should be cold, but I feel nothing. With a tinge of regret at my coming departure, I close my eyes; I cannot bear to look any longer. The river has me now - it will not be long. Goodbye my old friend - keep our secrets safe and sound.

THE VOICE IN THE ROOM

It was dark, so very dark – and quiet. The only sound was the faintest whisper of a breeze coming from somewhere, like the wind sighing as it caresses the leaves of a tree. The blackness in wherever he was – a room, a cell, a box – whatever, was total and sensory numbing, no light penetrated the gloom that he could make out. Why was he here? How did he get here? Many different questions started to crowd his mind, asking for answers that he could not give. The truth was - he did not really know who *he* himself was.

Amnesia? It was difficult to say, or to start speculating on his current situation. As it was, he did not feel in any great hurry to find out. There was a serenity about how he felt, a desire to stay in the moment, or rather, to deny the truth – whatever that truth was.

Feeling around, there was nothing. No furniture or walls – nothing that he could touch. Holding his arms directly out in front of his face, he moved them out in a sweeping motion – almost as if gesturing to a crowd. Thin air was all he found.

A sound off to the right – so slight he almost missed it. Again, it came – this time a little louder and closer to where he stood. Straining, he tried to pick out what it was, moving in the direction it had come from – shuffling so as not to go tumbling over some hidden obstacle.

Silence again – deathly silence. Then the breeze picked up and drowned out the noise – leaving him a little puzzled and a little frustrated.

Curious, he settled into the position he now found himself in and waited. Sure enough, it came again, and this time, it was right beneath him. It did seem quite muffled, but he was close enough to make out four words. "Mark, are you home?"

The name triggered something deep within the recesses of his mind and he found that a light was beginning to penetrate the murky gloom that was his memory. Footsteps now – he was sure of it. The sound echoed, as if the steps were heavy and on a hard surface – a wooden floor perhaps. Again, the name was called "Mark, where are you?" More urgent now, with maybe a touch of panic in the tone.

He tried to call out – managing to shout, "I am in here," as loud as he could. The person just carried on walking and calling out – obviously not hearing him. The owner of the heavy footsteps stopped directly below where he was now; he could hear breathing coming out in shallow gasps – then a creaking and a rattling as something heavy parted company with what held it and a weighty slam, as whatever it was made contact with the hard floor beneath.

A pause then, silence for a while – perhaps thirty seconds or so. It was almost as if the person below was contemplating – deciding what they should do. Footsteps once more, getting closer, the breathing a little heavier –

almost close enough now for him to reach out and touch. A buzzing sound halted the steps, a muffled cry of anguish and a sigh as a bleep echoed out, followed by the voice again. It sounded like a woman – now it was much closer and he could make it out, definitely a woman. She sounded vaguely familiar, as though he once knew her; in the distant past – maybe a thousand years ago - but he could not quite place her.

Listening intently, he tried to make out some of the words she was saying and managed to grasp a couple of them, "house" and "no sign". Who was she? What was she doing and what was she looking for? The voice stopped once again, and the footsteps resumed. A sound like a handle turning filled the silence. Once, twice, three times but no door opened. Whatever it was, it seemed that it was stuck.

Something jangled, was it keys? A loud snap as a lock slid, and then a creak as the door slowly swung open, allowing light to penetrate the gloom – rendering him unable to see clearly for a few seconds. It subsided and he made out the silhouette of a person standing in the doorway. It looked like a woman but from where he was, he could not quite tell. The light behind created a kind of corona around the figure.

He/she moved forward a step, hand slipping down the side of the door – searching for a light switch maybe. There was a curse, almost a whisper but he caught it, "where is the damn thing". It was definitely a woman's voice, soft and soothing. He wanted to reach out then, put his hand over hers, and tell her not to switch the light on. There was an urgency deep within that screamed at him to stay in the dark, to send her out, send her back down the steps and away from this place. It only held misery and heartache.

It was too late. Light flooded the room, finding every dark corner and alcove – revealing all the secrets that they held.

The woman was still for a few brief seconds, and then she screamed. It was a terrible sound, a haunting sound. Her hands found her face, nails digging into yielding flesh – drawing blood. He watched all this with a dawning realisation of what was happening. He did not want to look but was powerless to prevent it. Turning around, gazing back over his shoulder, he looked at what she was seeing.

Hanging from the rafters in the roof, toes hovering a few feet above the boarded out attic floor – was the body of a man. Staring transfixed, he felt himself drawn away from the scene in front of him – as if an invisible force was in control. The man hanging behind him, of course, was himself.

As he floated towards a blueish, white glowing speck in the distance, the screaming faded. The closer he got to it, the calmer he became - serene and peaceful. Although he felt sad, for the pain he was causing to the woman he was leaving behind – he knew it was the best thing he could have done. She would understand in time.

The last thing he heard – away in the distance now – before he passed through the light and into what lay beyond was his wife screaming his name, over and over.

WHAT HAPPENED LAST NIGHT

What happened last night? All I can remember is getting into the taxi to go into town – after that, nothing. No memories, no recollections, no glimmer of anything – zilch. My clothes are still on, even my shoes, which seem to be caked in mud - the bedsheets covered in it.

I have rummaged through my pockets – both in my jeans and my jacket, but there is no phone. My wallet is still there, along with a good selection of notes. The twenties stick out a little – being the biggest ones - and even *they* seem to have mud smeared all over them.

Looking around the room, all seems normal. The sun is shining through the window and it looks to be quite high in the sky – must be at least noon then. The curtains are open, letting the light clamour in, reflecting off the glass and not helping at all with the steady throb behind my eyes.

Where have I been to get in such a state? Fair enough, just lately I *have* been on quite a few benders, but nothing like this. This has never happened to me before and it is quite scary not to remember any of the previous evening.

Time to get up I think, although my legs feel like dead weights – as if someone has pumped them full of lead. It is a massive effort to swing them out of bed, letting gravity take over as each one thump down on the carpet with a bang. At this time, I do not trust myself to stand – knowing that to do so would result in the inevitable face-plant. In addition, my stomach feels a little unsteady and any sort of movement may see me lose its contents all over the floor.

I pause for a while, trying to bring my breathing under control and calm the storm that is currently raging deep in my guts. I can hear something. It sounds like a dripping sound, maybe a tap. It is quite consistent in its rhythm, plop, plop, plop.

This time, I *did* manage to rise to my feet, standing for a few seconds, swaying like a drunk, kicked out at last orders. One foot in front of the other that is the ticket – nice and steady, easy does it.

The landing outside the bedroom door is, perhaps, seven or eight strides away. Not far in the grand scheme of things, but with the situation being as it is – it feels like trying to scale Everest in flip-flops.

The door is most definitely my friend and saviour, I grasp at it for dear life, as a drowning man will do at a scrap of flotsam, bobbing around in the icy cold waters. A pause once again, thinking, what to do next? The dripping was louder now, and close by – just around the corner maybe, from the spare room?

The bathroom was on my left, the door ajar – letting in more of the midday sun, casting its warmth through the house. Dust motes dance before my eyes in the sunbeams that arrow across my path.

Leaving the bathroom behind, I shuffle along the short corridor that ends at the spare room – which seems to be the source of the noise. Drip, drip, drip, still it goes on. Now I am a little closer to the room, I can hear something else - quieter and more sinister. It sounds like someone breathing.

The banister is now on my left, and it provides a convenient stopping place to rest for a few seconds – to gather my thoughts.

Fragments of memory begin to filter through the fog, snatches of this and that – stood at a bar talking to the bar tender, eating pizza, waiting in line for a cab. Usual things you would expect. Then, something else slammed into focus and I almost let out a yelp.

To reach the stairs, I have to walk past the open spare room door. This does not fill me with glee, for I have an idea what, or who, might be in there. Still, pondering it would not get me out of here and so I manage to get my betraying legs to work again.

The sound of the dripping is loud now, echoing through the dark and empty halls of my mind, striking terror. Still moving, closer and closer still, a quarter of the room revealed itself to me, and then a third, half and finally I am standing looking in.

The breathing sound was coming from the man sat on the edge of the bed – facing away from me and staring out of the window seemingly. His hair looks dank and straggly, unwashed and greasy. He has no shirt – bare on his top half, his shoulder muscles bunched up as if tense – waiting to pounce. His arms look huge, biceps bulging.

The dripping was causing a pool to form on the wooden floor of the room, dark and sticky. The throat of the woman, slashed from ear to ear, reveals a dark open wound that looks like a yawning mouth. What is left of her face is as white and pure as a snowdrift untrodden. She is hanging by her ankles, upside down, from the trap door that leads to the loft space.

More memory continues to bombard me, even as I gaze over this monstrous scene, I begin to recall, to remember.

We ran through a field, trying to get away…from whom? From this crazy sat on the bed? I snatched the phone from the front pocket of my jeans – that bit is now clear. Then something hits me from behind and I go down. The woman was with me, she was screaming.

I look up once more, into the room and my gaze settles on the dead woman. My wife.

A gasp escapes me and the man slowly turns. I am stuck in a paralysis; legs welded to the floor. He is coming at me, teeth bared in a terrifying grin. Blood, caked around his mouth and chin, his torso covered in it. He moves swift, on legs clad only in a pair of shorts.

The front door is at the bottom of the stairs. Can I make it before he reaches me? Even if I do, will he catch me before I make it a hundred yards even?

I must try, at least. One foot in front of the other, legs are responding thank God, but he is behind me, I can hear. His breath is on my neck, halfway down the stairs, reaching out for the door handle. Please be unlocked. The last couple of stairs and I am there.

My hand turning, praying, hoping. It feels like an eternity, as if the handle itself is spinning, and I will never get to the end. Then, a click and the door swings open. I have made it! I start to move, one foot outside, one still in. The fresh air hits me like a mallet to the head, causing me to grimace against it. Still, I move and step over the threshold into the mid-day sun. Expecting a cruel hand to fall on my shoulder at any moment.

The hand does not come. I pause halfway down the path, my breathing laboured and painful, and chest hitching with the effort of drawing oxygen into my lungs. I chance a quick look over my shoulder and all I see is an empty path leading up to the open door – the dim light from inside making it look like the mouth of a cave. A dark and dangerous one, with maybe a big bad bear lurking inside.

I back up until my rump bumps against the gate, staying still – watching cautiously. After a moment or two, I feel things changing once again. Almost in a trance, my feet begin to take me back towards the house, towards the horror. I cannot seem to stop it.

Inside, it feels cooler than it had done before, calmer too. I close the door gently behind me and it locks itself on the Yale. Upstairs, the dripping has stopped. I walk through the kitchen, living room and utility room – no sign of anyone. The steps creak under my weight as I make my way upwards, each time; the noise seemed to shake the whole house – alerting whoever was waiting for me.

The spare room is empty – other than my wife, who continues to hang from the loft hatch, her eyes blank and lifeless. At least the blood had stopped dripping – for that, I am grateful.

The other rooms are also empty. I sit on the edge of the bathtub, memories returning with each passing second.

There was no man, no killer. I had seen him with my mind's eye, nothing more. I was running away from something, but it was not what I thought. No. I look down at myself, at my clothes covered in mud – only it is not mud is it.

I had killed my wife. I had done it with one of the knives from the kitchen drawer – the one with the serrated edge that we use for cutting up raw meat.

Why, I cannot even begin to say or to understand. I am crying - I can feel the tears rolling down my cheeks. There is a mirror above the sink facing me and I can see my reflection looking back. I don't recognise the man who stares at me, the blood streaked face, the wild-looking eyes and hair askew at every possible angle.

She will be waiting for me, I need to go to her, soon, before it is too late and she is lost forever.

I walk back to the spare room and pause at the door. Her eyes regard me with indifference. They are glazed over, half-lidded, making her look as if she was in the process of nodding off. I should join her – I am tired.

The knife is on the floor, by the bed. I can see the dark stains that cover the blade. The handle is sticky, but somehow comforting. I am going to sit on the bed now. I think it is time to go to sleep.

Epilogue 1

The news report stated that two bodies taken away this morning were a male and a female – believed to be married couple, John and Carol English. Police say that they have both sustained injuries consistent with a knife attack and that they are treating the deaths as suspicious.

Later – another report stated that 'John English, 36, an unemployed labourer, had a history of mental illness and had only recently spent a period of time at a mental health unit in York. Relatives are calling for an enquiry into why Mr English was deemed fit to return to his home when he 'clearly still had issues', the statement concluded.

2

"Are you excited," the young man said to his girlfriend, who stood by his heel, almost jumping around in her haste to get inside. They had bought the house for twenty thousand less than the asking price so had picked up a real bargain. The man unlocked the door and stepped inside, holding it open for his partner to follow. She gazed around at the empty spaces, visualising where the furniture would go.

They had waited almost five years to be in a position to buy, scrimping to save the deposit and then looking for the right house to come along. She had a feeling they would be happy here.

On the way to the kitchen, she heard something. At first, maybe it was just her imagination, but now she concentrated, it was clear. She stopped at the foot of the stairs, her head cocked to one side, listening. "Andy," she said, "What is that dripping noise?"

WAITING FOR THE NUMBER THIRTY-SIX BUS

The sky was a dark gunmetal grey colour, making it look ominous and potent as the rain clouds and thunderheads built up directly overhead. The roads and footpaths were still dry but soon enough, there would be rivers of water flowing along and into the drains that were dotted along at intervals. Simon gazed up, almost lost in his thoughts, not seeing or hearing the people sat around him, chattering to each other or looking at their phones – each one oblivious to him, as though he did not exist.

The man sat closest stood up, walked out onto the pavement, and stuck out his arm. He had a weary, worn look on his face, as though he had endured a thousand winters. His suit was blue with shiny patches just beginning to show on the seat and knees. The shoes that covered his feet were scuffed brown loafers and seemed a size too big.

The grumbling noise of an approaching engine grew in intensity, before a bus appeared and pulled up adjacent to the stop. The doors hissed as they swung open, letting off three passengers – who each wandered off in different directions. The man waited until they had cleared, and then stepped onto the bus, flashing his travel card to the driver who waved him on. With another hiss, the doors closed and the bus pulled out into traffic and was gone.

The remaining members of this particular bus stop gang now numbered seven. Simon waited patiently for the number thirty-six. It would be along soon but in the meantime, he watched, he listened.

Across the road from the bus stop was a park, with a few swings, a seesaw and a roundabout that had half of the framework missing. No children played on them, no parents watching them – it was a weekday morning and they would all be at school. A man with a dog walked across the grass, throwing a stick for it to chase after and retrieve. Other than that, it was deserted.

The dog was barking loudly at its owner – asking in the only way it could for the stick thrown once more. It was circling the man, tail wagging and tongue lolling out of the side of its mouth, looking every bit the happy companion. Man's best friend.

They both rounded the house that sat on the edge of the park, and disappeared from sight – leaving the grass deserted once more. There is something sad and desolate about a park with no one in it - lonely and devoid of the laughter and chatter that should be there. Simon lowered his head and stared at the cracked concrete between his feet - looking at a piece of old bubble gum, discarded and left for some unlucky soul to come along and step in. There were other things too, cigarette packs and tab ends, a crisp packet, a chocolate wrapper and the piece de resistance, a used condom.

Another bus came along – this time it was the number twenty – which dropped off no one but picked up the remaining six passengers (other than he of course). He lifted his head and watched it go with a heavy heart. They were his company after all, his gang. Now he was by himself, just one lonely man sitting on a bench inside a bus shelter that smelled sourly of urine, with a hardened piece of chewing gum at his feet.

Often, Simon had wondered what life would have been like had things been different, if his parents had brought him up with happiness and not as much in the way of punishment. More praise maybe, more love and tenderness. Still, no amount of dreaming or wishing would change anything. Of course, his parents were no longer able to hold him back and to admonish him. Those days were long gone.

Once, when he was five, he had peed the bed, awoken by a nightmare in which the bogyman chased him, slobbering chops, sharp teeth wanting to bite, to rip. The scream stuck in his throat and he could not be sure if he had done it aloud – although the spreading wetness between his legs meant that he would be the recipient of stern words when his parents found the sheets. Sure enough, he was beaten and forced to sleep in the unwashed bed for the next week. This was how his childhood was.

Yet another bus passed by, this one a single deck with only a handful of passengers on board. No one, it seemed, wanted to leave the bus at this particular stop and so it whizzed by leaving only the diminishing drone of the engine and the harsh, acrid smell of the diesel fumes behind.

The world was an unforgiving place – the strong would survive but the weak withered and died, fading away to nothing with not so much as a memory to keep them alive.

Even in death itself, a soul can wander for centuries – through hallways and highways, ghost towns and abandoned old houses, forever cursed and in limbo, searching - hoping.

Simon felt like that sometimes, especially between buses, when he was alone with his thoughts. He knew he was crazy. Did they not say though, that anyone who thinks they are sane are most probably crazy - and vice versa.

He glanced to the left, the shelter walls adorned with graffiti and adverts for holidays and life insurance (ha – that was ironic). They were grubby and lined with the dirt of the road, countless exhaust pipes spewing out tonnes of carbon. In the corner, tied up with twine, a small bunch of flowers clung desperately to life – the petals dropping off and the stems drooping. Placed there two weeks before, when they looked fresh and vibrant but now all that remained was death.

Simon has seen the woman tie them to the side of the shelter, before tucking a card inside and leaving quickly. She had seemed fidgety and nervous, casting suspicious looks left and right as she went about the task. Her eyes were red, from crying maybe and her hair looked dull and unwashed, tied up with a simple elastic band.

She had not returned since. The flowers were testament to that, with their desperate look and obvious neglect.

Lost in thought, Simon failed to notice the couple who had taken a seat each on the little bench inside the shelter – waiting for their ride. The man – perhaps thirty years old – picked out the card that was still nestled in between the stalks of the flowers, and read aloud the comments.

"Taken from us all too soon, rest in peace," he said. "Awww it's so sad," his partner replied. "So young he was too," she added. The man stood and walked to the edge of the pavement, the cars and trucks going by at speed, blowing up road dust into his face. "How could he have done it?" "He must have been at rock bottom to throw himself in front of a bus, the poor guy," he said as he slowly shook his head. "Simon, his name was I think".

Just then, the number thirty-six bus slowed to a halt in front of the stop and idled for a few moments before the driver opened the doors. The man and woman both climbed aboard and paid their fares, choosing seats in the middle of the bottom deck.

Simon followed and hopped onto the bus – only he shuffled straight by the driver, who did not acknowledge him, or protest even when he did not pay. Instead, he closed the doors and drove away, whistling a tune to himself and thinking about what he was having for dinner that night.

It was always the same seat for Simon – always the first one on the left. It gave him the best view. He would ride the route, and then disembark back at the stop – where he would once again, await the arrival of the number thirty-six bus.

FACE MASKS AT A FUNERAL

The cars – two of them – moved slowly down the long narrow drive that lead to the crematorium. One, a large black pick-up truck at the front, held three mourners, the other – a blue estate, had two.

A man was standing at the entrance to the small chapel, dressed in a crisp black suit with a startlingly white shirt, topped off with a simple thin black tie. His hands, clasped together behind his back as he awaited the arrival of the cars, fidgeted as his fingers twiddled idly, unseen by anyone other than a second man who stood just inside the vestibule, a thin smile touching the corners of his mouth.

The grounds basked in the sunshine, golden and warm. Shafts of light penetrated the treetops and touched the dewy grass underneath where the pots and flowers of countless cremations sat, alongside pictures of the deceased and messages on cards and paper. It was a beautiful scene, a sad scene. Either one could quite easily bring a tear to the eye.

Gently, both cars pulled up outside of the chapel and the doors opened, each one spilling out the occupant into the bright morning – five in all. There were three women and two men, all of whom were seemingly into their late fifties or early sixties. The youngest, one of the women, walked up to the man in the black suit and offered him a strained smile. She had dark brown hair tied up in a bun so it would fit nicely underneath the plain black hat she wore. From her pocket, she produced a facemask and slipped it on, as did the other four, and then followed the man in the black suit inside, away from the warmth of the day.

The chapel was dimly lit and cool. They walked side by side along a narrow corridor, which led into the main room, in which a number of chairs sat in rows of two. There were ten in all, each one two metres from the next. They were blue, with padded seats and backs, and in front of them, a small hymnbook and a pamphlet awaited it's user to pick it up and read the words printed within.

Soft music played from somewhere close by. Hidden speakers amplifying and sending out the mellow tunes to the gathered few. The song was by a folk band, one that the deceased had enjoyed listening to whilst in the final few years of his life, and which now was the focus of his widows grief.

They sat, followed by a short pause as the vicar arranged a few sheets of paper on the lectern at which he was standing. No one moved, and no one spoke. The music continued; soothing and melancholy, playing out the final few bars before the room fell silent.

At the back of the chapel, a man watched on, curious. The suit he wore – a dark blue – was immaculate and unblemished by creases or wear. The shoes on his feet were of the shiniest polished leather, reflecting brightly under the lights from the ceiling. He shuffled slightly from foot to foot as if agitated and nervous.

After clearing his throat loudly, the vicar began the service. Recollections of life, of love's, of laughter. He recounted several stories about the deceased, what he loved to do, his childhood, marriage, having children and on into later life and, ultimately, death itself.

The woman on the front row to the left was sobbing, her chest hitching, along with her shoulders as the words fell from the pages and drifted into the air for all to hear, to feel, to remember. The service continued, through a hymn, a poem and finally a short reading by the brother of the man in the coffin, which sat on a trestle table next to a hole in the wall – the front of which - draped tastefully by purple velvet curtains.

More music. This time a ballad of some sort, lots of violins and cello's. The sound punctuated the harshness of the grief and brought some smiles to go hand-in-hand with the tears. One by one, the five mourners walked to the front and spent a few moments touching the coffin, saying a few words, shedding a few more tears.

The man at the back of the room moved forward, gliding gracefully along the carpeted floor, until he stood just behind the last of the five. She was the widow, her hair, still pristine and tied into a bun under her hat, smelled faintly of shampoo. The man could smell it as he stood waiting – it provoked memories within him, stirring something from his dim and distant past.

She turned, her eyes full with the tears of grief and despair looking straight through him – and yet – she flinched for the briefest of moments. It was as if she had touched a static-charged surface and gasped, stepping back, before finding herself once more and turning to leave – following the others from the room.

The man took a step forward and glanced at the picture on the coffin lid. It was in a silver frame, interwoven with an intricate pattern of flowers and trees and mythical creatures. It was a beautiful piece. The man in the picture was a handsome looking fellow. Perhaps he was around fifty, perhaps a little younger. He was laughing, the woman with him, also laughing at something just out of shot. They both looked insanely happy and alive. The woman in the picture was the woman that had just left, walking out with her immediate family, crying the tears of grief that would be with her forever more. The man in the picture – well – the man in the picture smiled, running his finger over the photograph in its frame, tracing the smiling faces – feeling the love captured within this simple photo - and then he followed his wife outside into the mid-morning sunshine.

THE TEST

The car was an old blue Ford, sitting underneath the tree in the end bay of the car park. Janice glanced once more at her test candidate – eighteen years old, shoulder-length greasy hair and clothes that were in need of a wash. He had a swagger about him that spoke of attitude. She hoped and prayed it would be a smooth and easy test. So often, the ones with an edge would make for a tough forty minutes out on the road.

Janice had scanned the waiting room as she came out of the office door and called his name, "Jack Davis," her eyes finding the lad in the corner, looking like an extra from

'The Walking Dead'. She just knew it would be him, and sure enough, up popped the hand.

While he scanned the form and signed his name, she inwardly cursed. Today seemed to stretch away into the future like an endless highway, long and full of misery. She had woken feeling a little rough around the gills, a slow and thumping pain settling behind her eyes and threatening to spill out into a full-blown migraine. "Not today please," she muttered as the kettle boiled and clicked off, the toast popping up from the toaster at the exact same time.

Breakfast felt like a chore – the toast seeming to stick fast in the back of her throat and only disappearing with a little help from the coffee. Work was a necessity though, and so she showered and dressed as she had done thousands of times before, heading out of the front door and locking it behind her, driving into the test centre – almost on autopilot - ready for what the day would throw at her.

Watching her first candidate of the day sign his name at the bottom of the form, she wished dearly that she had just rolled over and gone back to sleep.

The car itself – for he was using his own for the test and not that of an instructor – was borderline scrap. He had produced the MOT certificate (which was in date and valid) so it was deemed roadworthy, although Janice doubted it would pass if tested today. Diligently, she checked the tyres for wear and the overall condition of the rest of the car (hoping to find a reason to refuse) before she would allow the test to go ahead. There was a small chip on the windscreen but it was towards the corner and not obscuring the view of the driver, or herself. Other than that, it was all OK.

"Can you read the number plate of that red car over there please," she said, pointing to an Audi parked on the main road. Jack read off the numbers and letters on the plate effortlessly. Once again, Janice inwardly cursed – hoping he would be unable to read it.

They both got into the car, Janice brushing crumbs and a crumpled up cigarette pack off the seat, before sliding in and buckling the seatbelt. She took him through the usual safety precautions and what he was to expect out on the test, before asking how he would check, and ensure the tyres were safe before starting a journey. All this was second nature to her, acting on pure habit alone this morning – the headache beginning to get worse. How badly she wanted this to be over and finished.

Jack smirked at her – as though this was a chore and he knew everything already after answering the question – again correctly. "Pull away when you are ready," she said to him.

The first ten minutes went by quickly, and without too much drama (for which she thanked the God's), and he did actually seem to be driving well.

After that – it all went downhill. Approaching a stop junction, he pulled out whilst the car was still rolling – a serious fault and a fail. Not long after, Janice had to grab the wheel and pull the car away from a certain collision with a parked vehicle on the opposite side of the road – again – another serious fault and a fail.

Jack noticed this and knew the test had gone away from him – the result an inevitable 'FAIL'. Rather than take the opportunity to relax and try to gain valuable experience, he became erratic and twitchy, taking risks and driving too fast.

"Slow down please," Janice asked. "You are above the speed limit for this road," she added. Jack barely seemed to hear her or register – instead, gaining speed and weaving in and out of traffic. "I am going to have to ask you to pull up at the side of the road at a convenient and safe place please," she said, a prickle of alarm now just settling deep in her guts. She did not like how this was going.

Up ahead, the road split into a dual carriageway, which led onto a motorway four miles further up the road. Jack headed for this and floored the accelerator and the car lurched quickly up to 70mph, and continued to rise. Janice gripped the door handle with all-out fear now. "Stop the car," she screamed. "Let me out".

Jack laughed, the car swerving across both lanes dangerously, the offside tyres mounting the grass verge in the middle of the road at one point – causing Janice to let out a yelp.

"You are not going anywhere," he said to her – looking sideways and leering. "You will get out when I say, and how I say". Janice was terror-stricken. She fumbled in her jacket pocket and brought out the mobile she kept in there. Jack noticed, and ripped it from her numb fingers, throwing it over his shoulder onto the back seat. "I don't think so," he laughed.

The car tore ever-quicker down the road. Janice began to cry as she pleaded with him to pull over. "Please, I won't say anything, I will walk back and you can drive home, just let me out".

In an instructor car, she could have used the dual control pedals to stop but in the learners own car – this was not an option. They now hurtled along at ninety miles per hour, the houses and side roads whizzing past as she hung onto the door handle for dear life.

They approached a roundabout – maybe a quarter mile ahead – and Jack actually *did* slow a little, but not enough. The island loomed large in the windscreen, filling it almost, before he pulled hard on the steering wheel and sent the car careering sideways around the outside lane – spinning around 360 degrees, and causing Janice to scream as the g-force took hold – before finally righting itself and on they went.

Janice was on the verge of hysterics, and Jack loved every minute of it. The look on his face was one of a young child who delights in torturing animals, watching a crane fly roll around – unable to move with its legs pulled off. The deep-seated glee he was experiencing was total and all consuming.

The direction they were travelling in would eventually bring them out into the town centre. Maybe, Janice thought, that might slow him down enough and give her a chance to escape.

She knew these roads intimately – having driven them thousands of times over the years, so she had an inclination that the route he was taking would snarl up with school traffic. God, I hope there are no kids about, she thought. The school will be busy.

The road bent slightly to the left, angling ever closer to the town centre. The speed was a constant ninety and the driving very erratic. Janice tried to clear her mind and focus on the task of getting away from this lunatic. If she panicked now – it might be disastrous.

"There's a school coming up," she said to him, trying to remain as calm as she could and not to let him think she was plotting. "You need to slow down in case a child runs out into the road – you won't have time to stop," she added.

The leer remained on his face – impassive almost – it was as if he had not heard, or did not want to listen. Either way, it was clear his intention was to cause as much destruction as possible, and maybe die trying. The thought sent fresh alarm racing through her, and it was difficult to keep it concealed – to disguise it. Sweat was running down her back in rivers, she could feel its clamminess against her skin – the blouse she wore sticking uncomfortably.

"Why are you doing this," she pleaded. Without turning, he replied, "what's the point, I've failed anyway, might as well go out in style".

"Who said you have failed, you might still pass if you pull over – we can talk it through," she said. "You must think I'm stupid," he screamed out – spittle flying from his mouth and spraying the dash. "All you want to do is get away, so you will tell me anything".

"You don't want to do this," she said again, "You can take your test again in a few weeks and everything will be fine. Just think about what you are doing here," she almost panted as the last of the words came out. The headache and the lethargy she felt this morning, forgotten, instead replaced by a survival instinct.

The stoplights in the distance, that marked the edge of town, were stuck on red. The car showed no signs of slowing or taking a different path – just flying headlong into oblivion.

Two other cars sat waiting for the lights to turn green, and Jack swerved around them and shot straight through the intersection, just missing the front bumper of a delivery van coming across the junction from the left. Horns blared and brakes screeched as the inevitable crash, avoided by mere millimetres, averted. "STOP" Janice screamed, "For God's sake stop," desperately trying to unlock the door.

The school was coming up fast on their left hand side – her side – and the panic set in once more. She could see kids crossing the road like a line of ants – the road safety warden, standing to attention with the lollipop pole grasped in her hands.

The woman looked up, hearing the noise of the engine and spotted the car moving at speed. The kids had spread out in a line of maybe ten or twelve across the road and she shouted for them to go back – grabbing the nearest few that she could reach. It would be too late, she thought, they didn't realise the danger, they would be mown down.

"Go back," she shouted across to them. "Quickly – a car is coming!" A few parents ran for their children and rough handed them away from the side of the road, and a few called out to them. They could all now see the danger that was fast approaching.

Janice acted purely on instinct. She grabbed the wheel with both hands and pulled as hard as she could, driving the car towards the nearside kerb and heading for a stand of trees that sheltered a few park benches and a small duck pond. Jack fought back, but the element of surprise had gained her just the slightest of advantages and she managed to keep the car on its present course.

The tyres screamed as they tore across the tarmac and mounted the kerb. Jack took one hand off the steering wheel and aimed a punch at her face – connecting squarely on the bridge of her nose and shattering it. Blood sprayed out from it, covering the windscreen and dash. The car bumped along the pavement, Jack trying to wrestle back control, before it collided broadside with a parked car and flipped over into the air at better than sixty miles per hour.

It rebounded off the first tree, smashed head on into the second tree, and came to rest on its roof in the duck pond, the tyres still rotating and the engine spluttering before eventually dying and cutting out.

Somewhere deep down in her subconscious, Janice was aware of a coldness seeping into her bones. It felt soothing. Sounds began to pierce the membrane that enclosed her mind, trickling, creaking, and crackling. Other noises, more persistent and urgent crowded in. There were what sounded like people shouting and splashing maybe?

Then, rough hands were pulling at her – she could feel them on her arms and legs. A shattering sounds, and many tiny pieces of glass rained down on her upturned face making her close her eyes involuntary against them.

"It's on fire," someone yelled from close by. "We need to get them out quick, there isn't much time," another voice shouted. Janice found herself lifted away and out of the car. Her mind had returned fully and she remembered everything. She twisted in the grasp of two men, who carried her to the edge of the pond and set her down carefully. "There's someone else in there," she said.

The men turned to wade back out to the stricken car when a loud 'whup' sound filled the air. People dived for cover as pieces of metal and glass shot out in a hundred different directions (the police would later find a number plate over a quarter of a mile away in someone's garden).

The heat was intense and Janice shrank back from it. The two men had thrown themselves beneath the surface, and now came back up – water dripping from them, eyes wide with shock. More people had joined at the edge of the water, and all looked on with horror as the car burned – sparks sizzling as they jumped and hit the water.

No one else would be leaving the car alive.

Janice suffered a broken collarbone and a fractured ankle. She was away from work for six months, suffering both physically, and mentally. Her recuperation was long and arduous, with times where she felt the end would never be in site. Jack, it turned out afterwards, was in the throes of drug abuse and had a history of mental issues – many of which involved violence. The police admitted that he should never have been behind the wheel of a car, and notes from his GP suggested that many of his problems stemmed from a broken home, abuse from his parents (several instances of fractured bones and bruising throughout his childhood) and his apparent isolation from school since the age of fourteen.

In the end, a recommendation for psychiatric intervention had gone unheeded, as had the social services reports – which outline systemic failures in picking up all the classic signs. Jack Davis killed himself. It was always going to come down to it – one way or another. The fact that he had tried to take others with him meant a deep-rooted psychosis went undetected.

It was by the grace of God (and the quick thinking of the driving examiner) that prevented an all-out catastrophe.

A year later, a woman stood quietly by the graveside of a young boy killed in a car crash. The grave was a simple one, a covering of grass that was a little too overgrown but devoid of flowers. The headstone was as simple as the rest of it, a few words with a birth and death date. That was all. Not much for a young life taken in turmoil.

The woman bent slowly – her ankle gave her pain on cold days like today – and placed a small bunch of flowers into a vase she had brought along, sitting it upright next to the headstone. She lingered a while, before walking away

– the breeze ruffling her hair and sending the autumn leaves swirling around her feet as she went.

SWEET DREAMS

After dark, when the lights are no longer illuminating, the world sleeps - and the world dreams. Some are good dreams, ones that leave a smile on waking, others though, well they are the ones that leave an indelible mark on us all. These are ones that, within our subconscious, we do not remember or recall in the waking hours – but instead are assailed by them when we close our eyes and give ourselves up to sleep.

He was having one of those dreams right now, she watched him toss and turn on his side of the bed – fighting with whoever or whatever was running around his mind. A bead of sweat was rolling down his forehead. She watched it with interest, making its way to the bridge of the nose, then off to the side, before falling, and onto the pillow.

She felt pity then, not the pity that you feel when you witness someone in peril or strife – no. This pity was born out of frustration and anger. That and what would inevitably come in the not-too-distant future.

His breathing hitched and then steadied out, mouth open as if trying to catch a fly (which is something her mother used to say to her as a child). She closed her own eyes, knowing that sleep would not come; it never did – not anymore. Once it got inside your head – the knowing and expectation – sleep was an impossibility.

As if on cue, he closed his mouth and began to snore. Quietly at first – more like heavy breathing really – but it steadily grew in volume, and would so even more as the night wore on.

She did not bother trying to nudge him, or move his position – as she had done countless times over years. Tonight there was no point.

Unusually, she had fussed over him at dinner, asking him what he wanted to eat and then preparing it, along with a cold bottle of his favourite beer. He had eaten it in relative silence, grunting every now and then as he replied to something she said. Afterwards, she had cleared the dishes away and then climbed the stairs to the bathroom, to shower and get ready for bed.

It was almost midnight before he collapsed into bed, having finished off the six bottles that remained in the fridge. She could smell the alcohol on him as it wafted across to her side of the bed. He was asleep in minutes.

Now, almost three hours later, she lay sleepless – listening to him snore. Listening to the sound that had accompanied her marriage for twenty-six years, for good and for bad, for richer and for poorer.

The drugs had not been difficult to get hold of – not when you knew the right people. They had been stored at the back of the medicine cabinet for weeks while she decided what to do, behind a tube of steroid cream and an old tin of deodorant that no one will ever use – bought as a Christmas present from someone or other years ago.

They were only really sleeping pills anyway – nothing hard-core or sinister. They would do the job she wanted from them though. Afterwards, well, afterwards it did not matter. What did matter was the task in hand. It had been long enough, it had been three hours and the time had come.

Looking at him once more, gazing down at him, propped up on her elbows, did she feel love? Once, a million years ago, they both loved each other with an intensity she did not think possible. Now, time had eroded that love until all that remained was pity. Deep down, in the depths of her soul though, the love still clung on desperately, and possibly always would. Tucked away as it was, deep in the recesses – much as the sleeping pills were in the medicine cabinet – it seemed as distant now as it ever had done.

Grasping the pillow she had retrieved from the storage cupboard, she lifted, paused for just a fraction of a second, and then placed it over his face.

At first, nothing happened. He carried on sleeping and snoring. Slowly, she applied more pressure until she could feel his body twitch. The breathing was becoming more laboured, breath struggling to get in, or out. There would be no fight in him – the drugs would do their job.

Surprisingly, it took almost six minutes for him to die. She had heard somewhere that it can take up to seven or eight minutes for a healthy human to suffocate – contrary to what you see in the films and on television. Five minutes and forty-three seconds though is what she counted out.

When she was sure it was over – she gently removed the pillow and looked at him. His eyes were closed and peaceful, lips slightly apart and just the very tip of his tongue visible out of the side of his mouth. He looked to her in that very moment, like the man she had married, a handsome man whom she loved and whom loved her back. He looked at peace.

With a sigh, she stood and walked across to the cupboard and replaced the pillow gently back onto the shelf. Returning to bed, she laid down and pulled the covers up to her chin – shivering a little at the chill.

Sleep was a long way from her mind, as far away as anything could be. Thoughts crowded in, battering and braying at her, to have their say – accusing and berating.

She thought that it would be a long, long time before she slept again.

Five minutes later, she was breathing deeply, breathing gently and fast asleep, snoring ever so quietly. Sleeping the sleep of the dead.

26 PRIMROSE STREET

The address on the slip of paper said twenty six Primrose Street, then underneath it in scruffy writing, 'last house on the left'. They had been given it by the man they arranged to meet up with, who passed on a small bunch of keys with a tag tied to them with a piece of twine. It was to be their temporary home before they could find somewhere a bit more permanent and now, rounding the corner at the bottom of the road, they started up the slight incline towards where the house stood.

The door was a faded blue, with paint that looked like it was in need of a fresh coat – it was sun bleached and starting to crack and blister. Not the usual sort of door but more an old-fashioned type, one with a big brass handle and matching letterbox and it looked very sturdy. The path leading up to it typified the rest of the house – rustic and charming, if a little run down.

Christine and Paul were new in the village, looking for that age-old 'rural retreat', away from the rat race of city living – hoping to recharge and refresh and to put as much distance between themselves and the life they had left behind. They had seen many properties but needed something quick and had stumbled upon this one in an advert in the local post office. The short note that had accompanied the blurry picture, promised them a home to move into immediately and with no upfront costs.

Now, as Paul pushed the front door open, and stepped inside, it did not seem to be their best decision. The air in the hallway, smelled rank as if something had died within its depths long ago, rotting in the heat of the sealed up house. Christine wrinkled her nose up at it and whispered "yuk" under her breath, huddling closer to Paul as they walked down towards an open door at the end of the corridor – presumably the kitchen.

The room – sparsely furnished with just a washing machine, fridge and a plain wooden table in the middle of the floor, along with two folding chairs tucked away under it - seemed in keeping with the outside. The large window, set into the far wall, looked out onto an overgrown narrow garden that stretched away to what looked like a pond at the bottom.

"This is awful," Christine said to him as she gazed out at the dense undergrowth. "It feels as though it has not been lived in for years". "It just needs a tidy up and we can have it looking how we want in no time," Paul replied. Inside though, he was already regretting taking the keys.

Paul trotted back out to the car and started to unload their things, which was not that much really, most of what they had brought with them was in storage. Once they had emptied the car, they both sat on the tired old settee that was against the wall in the living room. As with just about everything else, it looked as if there was not much life left in it but worn out as they both were, past caring. Christine put her head on Paul's shoulder and they rested, talking about their plans for the future – which did not include this house.

That evening as they both lay quietly in bed, listening to the wind howl around the creaking old eaves; it was difficult to imagine that they could be happy here, that they had made the right move by leaving the city and upping sticks. Things always seem at their worst at night though, Paul thought. Let us give it time, see how we go.

At some point during the night, Christine awoke and pulled the bed sheets up to her chin – shivering as the cold penetrated her and seeped down into her bones. Glancing over at Paul, she could see the steady rise and fall of his breathing as he slept soundly. Had she heard something?

She was sure she had – or maybe it was just her imagination. Listening intently, she strained to hear, trying to pick out any sounds over the wail of the wind. Nothing. Dismissing it, Christine closed her eyes.

This time, it was definite. A scraping noise, followed by a bump. She sat up in bed, head cocked. What was it? It seemed to be coming from above them – in the attic. Mildly alarmed now, she nudged Paul in the ribs, "Paul, wake up, I can hear something". "Whaaa, Paul said in a croaking, sleep fuelled voice. "There's something in the attic, I can hear it moving". "It's just the wind, go back to sleep – I will have a look in the morning," he moaned. He rolled over onto his side and resumed his sleep, leaving Christine wide-awake and sat bolt upright.

There was no chance of her dropping back off now, so instead, she lay arrow-straight with the quilt over her eyes, trembling – and not only due to the cold.

The next morning, it seemed to her that it was all daft and stupid – nothing could be up there. Nevertheless, she broached the subject with Paul as they tucked into their breakfast of eggs and bacon. "Will you go up and have a look," she said in-between mouthfuls, trying not to sound too upset and scared. Paul agreed he would – straight after they had finished eating.

The ladder that led to the attic was old and looked as though it might snap with even the slightest weight put on it. Paul eyed it suspiciously, not wanting to come tumbling down, breaking his neck – that would be just his luck. It slid down in its runner smoothly enough, with just the faintest squeal as the wood groaned at the movement.

Cautiously, Paul ascended one rung at a time, pausing on each one to test the strength, before moving onto the next. The trapdoor was latched but no lock, so it opened without much trouble, swinging back to reveal the gloom behind it, a darkness that was sinister and chilling. Paul looked back at Christine, who stared back, a grimace on her face. Turning, he took the final step and into the abyss.

The smell hit him first, much like the day before on walking into the house for the first time – only now, it was much worse, it was feral and hideous. Every part of him wanted to turn and flee, he was badly scared and the hairs of his arms were on end, as if sensing danger. The first step he took intensified the stench, almost making his eyes water. His hand went to his nose involuntary to try to cover the smell but it did little to effect it, it seemed to permeate through his skin, attacking every pore.

On he went, further into the attic, further into the formidable silence. The steps he took were short and jerky, afraid of tripping on some unseen obstacle, and he held his arms out in front for balance – and to prevent walking straight into something.

A noise then. Gone as quick as it came, a whispery sort of sound, and then a wet slithering as something moved. Paul stood rigid, trying to hear but picking up nothing. It was almost as if the noise was inside his head.

Somehow, he managed to move his feet and venture further in, digging out his mobile phone and switching on the torch. The weak light did not show him much, a jumble of old books, magazines and items of furniture piled here and there. The smell was getting stronger the closer to the far wall he was, making him gag a little. He considered going back but curiosity was overriding the fear and it forced him to go on.

A brief reflection caught his eye from just behind an old table, glinting from his torchlight. Moving cautiously, he started towards it, mindful that he might have to turn tail and run at any minute. The voice when it came froze him solid. His guts shrivelled up inside and he felt his bladder loose off and then the warm feeling as it ran down his leg.

"Yessss," it hissed. A simple word with a terrible undertone. The feet within his shoes felt as if they had swollen to the size of bricks and they would not move – he was stuck. The slimy, slithering sound again, like a gigantic slug dragging itself across the floor – coming for him.

Paul tried to scream but no sound came out. The creature slid out from behind the table and stared at him. It was like nothing he had ever seen, even in the depths of his nightmares. It came on, not on legs but on long viscous tentacles – which reached out, hunting him, and yearning for him. It had a leer on whatever passed for its face – a terrifying sight that struck him numb. It was closer now, eating up the ground quickly, bringing the foul stench with it.

Finally, he managed to get his feet to move – shuffling clumsily across to a pile of old magazines. The thing changed its course and followed, slobbering and drooling as it watched him go. Paul realised his mistake then, it had moved into position in-between him and the trap door.

It came on faster, closing the distance and hemming him in. Panic started to set in and his pulse was racing – heart hammering, sweat running down his face. It sensed the fear emanating from him in waves and this intensified its efforts. Paul made one last attempt to side step and run but his foot slipped on a newspaper and he went down in a tangle of limbs.

It was over quickly, one tentacle wrapping itself around his neck and constricting, snapping off his head - which rolled off and settled against a chair leg. The rest of him was absorbed into the creature bit by bit, almost as if he was becoming part of it. A sigh came from it, one of satisfaction. It glowed brightly, blinding in the gloom and illuminating everything around it.

From below, Christine called out, "What was that, did you fall?" Only silence greeted her. Concerned, she moved to the ladder and called out again, with the same response – or lack of it, just the steady hum of the wind and the tinny sound of the TV from the living room below.

A voice drifted down to her then, calling her up. It was Paul's voice, although to her it sounded a little strange –

maybe it was the acoustics up there. She placed her foot on the bottom rung and began to climb.

Reaching the top, she swung her leg around and stood up, looking around. There was no sign of Paul. Walking forward, she called out his name, mild alarm rapidly turning to all out panic. Was he hiding from her? Just then, a movement off to her left and slightly behind. She swivelled around quickly, ready to scold him for being childish, to grab him by the hand and get out of here as quickly as they could.

The thing that was before her was not Paul, she did not really know what it was, what she was seeing. Her brain cried out to her to run, to hide – anything but just do not stare at it. However hard she tried though, there was no way she could break the trance it held her in, no way of ripping her gaze away from it.

It began to move towards her, a mass of gelatinous terror that seemed to change shape and evolve in front of her eyes. One second, it looked hideous, the next, it looked like Paul. Then it would change back again. She could see arms and legs within its mass, which seemed to be dressed in Paul's clothes. A long tentacle reached out and caressed her cheek. Christine screamed.

Down in the living room, the TV continued to play to itself. The only other sounds in the house were the cracking and snapping of something loud from above. Bones perhaps.

Two weeks later, a young, good-looking couple walked up the path, which led to a faded blue door. The man, taking a bunch of keys from his pocket, stepped forward and unlocked it, pushing it open and entering the gloomy hallway beyond. His young wife followed him in, closing the door behind her. She stopped, head slightly tilted upwards, nose wrinkled as if sensing something bad, something terrible.

"What is that smell," she said.

A STORY BY THE CAMPFIRE

The ground underfoot was soft and yielding, cushioned with the ferns and moss that covered most of the forest floor. The sun just about penetrated the thick canopy above, letting the weak light filter through and cast its patterns and shapes – beautiful and mesmerising.

It was a warm day, even with the protection of the trees. The temperature sat at a lofty twenty-six degrees, as early as it was, and it promised to touch thirty or more by noon. Dust motes danced hypnotically in the sunbeams, as if they alone occupied this wonderful, enchanting place – dancing and celebrating in the only way they knew how.

Here and there, life would show itself, a bird would fly low, staying close to the ground – a woodcock or a snipe possibly – trying to avoid the deathly gaze of a hawk. A fallow deer poked its nose out from the foliage, sniffing the air, before turning tail and bolting through the trees to safety. Butterflies flitted from flower to flower on wings that defied nature, a blur to the naked eye, their colours and patterns miraculous.

It was the picture of serenity, almost as if it was the only place left on earth, a Garden of Eden.

Aaron continued his steady progress, being careful not to step on anything living, and watching out for deadfalls or hollows whereby one could easily break an ankle. He glanced at the watch on his wrist; a GPS tracker - bought as a gift by his parents for his birthday – the digital clock dial told him it was a little after 10am. The day would be long, but worthwhile – the journey across this part of the country was as stunning as you could find anywhere in the world.

A gap in the trees allowed him to spot the mountains in the distance, the snow-capped peaks shrouded in wispy cloud, like cotton wool that seemed to cling to the tops like a magnet to metal. An eagle soared directly overhead, its massive wingspan seeming to stretch to an inconceivable size. From this far away, Aaron found it difficult to pinpoint the exact species – although it was most likely an Osprey, or maybe a Golden Eagle.

He dabbed at his forehead with the sleeve of the shirt he was wearing, the sweat was beading as the ground began to slope upwards ever so slightly the closer to the foothills he got – raising his exertions with it. A bottle attached to the bottom of the pack he was wearing offered a cool drink to quench his developing thirst. He stashed it back after taking three mouthfuls – mindful that he would need to conserve what he had until he found a water source – maybe another fifteen miles of ever-rising terrain before that happened, at the place he intended to camp for the night.

After stowing away the camping equipment earlier, safely stored in his pack, Aaron had set out on the biggest leg of the trek – the one that would take him from the lakes region, through the towering forests, onto the foothills and the mountain slopes. It could be as long as three, or even four days depending on the weather and the walking conditions. He felt in good spirits though, and had a spring to his step as the narrow track disappeared behind him with each passing minute.

The weather app on his tracker warned that a front could come in before dark, bringing heavy rain and the possibility of thunderstorms. If that happened, the tent would come out quickly and he would find cover. As it was, the sun was still bright and warm – rain felt a million miles away.

As he walked, his mind wandered – thinking of all the decisions, all the mistakes, all the consequences of the actions he had taken. The reason he was here in the first place was a result of a failed relationship, a failed job and – in all honesty – a failed life. This was his sanctuary, his way out of the stress and the responsibilities that came with it all.

The choice was not an easy one. To walk away from a well-paid role was difficult and very much a gamble – one that Aaron felt was worth taking. Now, he was here, alone with his thoughts in this place of beauty, surrounded by the sights and sounds of nature with the next eighteen months stretching away into the distance.

A noise broke the spell that held him, a rustling in the undergrowth off to his right. He paused, watching intently for the creature that made it, guessing at a rabbit. Instead, a red squirrel hopped out onto the path in front of him, poised in a stance of wariness. It took a leap back into the brambles and appeared on the trunk of a big towering spruce, scampering up high and away into the canopy. Aaron afforded himself a smile.

As the morning wore on, the clouds that he could see were gathering and growing dark. The storm that promised to arrive looked to be building ready for the fireworks later on. Aaron quickened his step and marched on towards an area that he knew on the map, and satellite images, opened out into a small clearing with scattered boulders and tree stumps. This would be his home for the night.

The heat intensified with each step it seemed, reaching, and then overtaking the 30-degree mark. His shirt was soaked and stuck to his back uncomfortably; at times, the sun beat down mercilessly, baking his exposed skin and turning it an alarming shade of red. Then, thankfully, the sun disappeared behind one of the many clouds, or was hidden by the trees and provided some respite from the relentless rays.

Morning turned into afternoon and Aaron was beginning to flag, the incessant heat and humidity taking its toll. Up ahead, he spotted a slight rise and then heard the unmistakeable bubbling sound of water. He followed the noise through the trees for a hundred yards until he stepped out onto the banks of a stream. The water was flowing fast over the rocks and pebbles that sat on the streambed, causing it to froth and gurgle its way along the narrow strip of water, on its journey to meet the lakes far below.

Aaron dropped the pack and collapsed to the ground, taking a few minutes to recover and rest up. The overhanging branches provided some much-needed shade and he was quietly pleased with himself – more by luck than judgement – that he had found this.

Bending over, he dipped his head under the water and felt the cold immediately hit him, causing an involuntary gasp. The chill struck him between the eyes and he had a moment or two of brain-freeze, squinting down hard against it until it had passed. He felt better, cooled off and a bit less lethargic. Looking around, the stream meandered from around a corner to his left, flowing by where he sat, and off around another bend to the right. The noises of nature filled his ears – birdsong, insects buzzing around, small mammals scurrying through the undergrowth and even fish in the stream – he spotted a small silver flash as one rose to the surface, mouth wide open, snatching an unsuspecting water skater before disappearing once more into the depths.

Overhead, the clouds continued to intensify and grow ever darker - the heat growing with it. Aaron lent back against the trunk of the tree closest to him and slid down, his rump finding relief in rest as it settled against the mossy ground.

The first drop landed on his upturned face, causing him to blink against it. The rain, it seemed, wanted to come early – much earlier than the app on his phone had suggested. The coolness felt good against the clamminess of his skin, welcoming and refreshing.

The drops became persistent, falling in vertical curtains that obscured the landscape – before turning into a torrent. The wind swirled as the storm hit and took hold – the calm and heat of just a few minutes earlier gone and forgotten. Aaron huddled under the overhang of a stand of trees a little away from the stream and began digging out the camping gear. This – apparently – was as far as he would go today.

The tent was a pop-up one, and inflated with ease. Small enough to fit snuggly underneath the lowest branches of the trees, it would offer him the protection from the downpour and the storm that was now raging.

Aaron quickly stowed his equipment inside the tent to prevent them from being saturated, and he followed behind, zipping the front flap securely to the bottom.

The sides bellied in as the wind buffeted and howled around the small two-man tent, but he was dry and happy enough to wait it out. It was the first bad weather on the trek so far, which was lucky and fortunate given he was so close to the mountains.

The weather outside the thin walls continued to rage and worsen as the day wore on into the late afternoon, and even beyond that into the evening. Aaron read a book to pass the time – an action adventure about pirates on the high seas. It captured his imagination and thrill for seeking out new places – travelling and exploring. When he finally put it down – his bladder screaming in protest – it was well past eight o'clock, and the rain continued to fall.

Unzipping the flap, he peered out into the darkening gloom. It should stay light for at least another couple of hours, he thought, but the storm had brought darkness early and it felt as if it were the closing embers of the day, with midnight just around the corner.

He darted quickly across to the nearest tree and undid his tracksuit bottoms to urinate. This in itself was a difficult task with the wind threatening to return the stream back from whence it came. The trick was to lean forward with legs wide apart, trying to stay as low to the ground as possible. It was a real skill. Finished, he made the short few steps back to the safety of the tent and ducked inside, zipping down firmly behind himself.

Tiredness seeped deep into his bones, the shock of fresh air and wind had knocked the life from him. Before long, the feeling of sleep stole in and Aaron was snoring quietly - all around the storm battered the trees sending branches flying and whipping up the water from the stream, sending it high into the air in plumes of spray.

At some point during the night, the wind abated and calmed. The storm had done its worst and was now moving on to pastures new, heading across the mountain range to the coast far off into the distance, and over to the many isles that dotted the dark water like tiny oasis in the vastness of the great ocean.

Aaron woke, checking his watch and seeing the illuminous dial stare back at him showing the time at a little after two in the morning. The wind was no more, the tent sat unmoving, the sides flat and unruffled. Somewhere close by, Aaron could hear a crackling sound, like twigs snapping. He listened; head cocked to one side trying to pick out the direction it was coming from.

Curious, he poked his head outside the tent. Immediately the cool night breeze set to work on making his teeth chatter. The sky was clear and the billions of stars that stretched out across the Milky Way shone bright and wondrous. He could make out the clusters and spirals within it, bunched close together making it look like churned milk – the reason for the name.

The noise appeared to be coming from beyond the trees on the opposite site of the main trail - Aaron could just make out shapes in the moonlight – a dark mass, about fifty yards away. A glow radiated out from the same place, flickering and dancing in the shadows. A fire?

Careful to hide his presence from whoever was out there, he slipped out of the tent and crept across the open ground to the cover of pine and spruce that blanketed most of the area.

Aaron leant against the trunk of a tree and peered around it in the direction of the light. Up ahead – no more than twenty or thirty yards – a small campfire was burning. The structure was a good couple of feet off the ground - built up using boulders and stones (from the stream?) and was giving off enough heat for him to feel it from where he stood. A pile of wood sat close by, waiting for the flames to wane and die down.

On the far side of the fire – facing his direction – sat an old man. The dancing flames made his face look ablaze and his eyes alive with light. He had thick grey hair, which came down below the shoulder blades and a long knotted beard. From what he could see, the man wore a thick wool jacket, dirty looking pants and big sturdy walking boots. The skin on his face looked weathered with the passing of time; deep runnels cut through the flesh around the mouth and eyes – making him look ancient.

Aaron watched him for a few minutes – wondering what to do – when, clearly and with a voice that sounded much younger than his face suggested, the old man said "why don't you come on over and take a pew?"

Aaron was taken aback for a moment – how did he know he was here - he was hidden from view and he had made no noise. Heart beating a little faster than he was used to, he stepped out from the cover of the tree and into full view.

The heat from the fire intensified and he felt the need to sit next to it and warm up. "Come," the man said, and motioned with his hands to a spot opposite where he sat. Aaron walked slowly, still a little wary of this stranger out in the wilderness – although he supposed that to the man by the fire, that's exactly what *he* was too.

A small tree stump made a perfect stool to sit on, right in front of the flames. The warmth it spread through his bones was welcoming and pleasant. Aaron sat on the dead stump and began rubbing his hands together. "I am Wilf," the old man said, "pleased to make your acquaintance". "I don't tend to see folks this far up into the forest". He eyed Aaron with an amused look in his eyes; they twinkled in the firelight, making them seem mischievous. "My name is Aaron, pleased to meet you too Wilf. I am hiking up to the foothills and the storm forced me to camp early," he said, "Although looking at the skies now, it's like it never happened".

"Up here, this close to the mountains, the weather can be subtle and cruel in equal measures. It can hit you when you least expect it and cause you nothing but trouble," Wilf said, speaking slowly and concisely. "Many a traveller has come to grief in the storms, it's a kind of occupational hazard for me, I am used to it," he said as he shook his head and chuckled.

"What brings you up here?" Aaron asked, leaning forward slightly to hear him better over the crackle of the fire.

"Oh I am just here," he replied. "I move from place to place, sometimes staying for a while, sometimes moving on quickly, it depends on how I feel at the time".

"So you live out here?" Aaron enquired, genuinely interested now.

"I do, yes. More years than I care to remember".

"There was a time – many moons ago, back when I was a strapping young man – one that could have taken on the world – and won. I was eager and quick fast, always wanting to step out into the unknown and try new things – it was a trait of mine that got me into a few scrapes I can tell you," he laughed.

"Word was, an old tin miner had come across gold in the stream," he pointed through the trees to where the tent was.

"The spring comes from the tallest peak you can see, right at the top almost, and tumbles all the way down, past where we are now, and spills out into the first big lake down there." He paused to hawk and spit on the ground next to his feet, before continuing. "I was young like I said, the lure of gold was too much and I headed on up here seeking out the fortune that was promised".

"What happened?" Aaron asked.

"Well – I certainly did not get rich," he laughed, head thrown back in a hearty bellow which quickly turned into a coughing fit". He bent over – head between his legs and hacked away for a few minutes, until he could get himself under control again.

"No, there was no 'gold rush' like you hear about, with big nuggets just tumbling out of the mountain side," he said, whilst wiping tears from his eyes, brought on by the coughing fit.

"The prospectors just drifted away in time – once they realised that it was all just a crock of horse shit". The old man's gaze turned upwards, towards the mountains in the distance and he sighed – a sad and lonely sound.

"I stayed. I guess it just became my home – where I felt most comfortable and alive. The outdoors and the fresh air can call to a man; can whisper sweet nothings in his ear, as if a woman is calling with the promise of tenderness".

Aaron studied his face, with all its weathered lines – each with its own story to tell no doubt, and wondered just how old he was. He looked to be at least a hundred – although this couldn't be so – surely not. How could he survive out here? Still, there was something antiquated about him, even down to the clothes he wore, which seemed to be as old as he was.

The fire crackled on, sending sparks flying into the air each time the breeze gusted through the flames. The heat was soothing and he could feel himself nodding as he sat, listening to Wilf talk. An owl hooted from somewhere close by, followed by a flap of wings as it took to the air, up into the clear night sky.

"There was a time where a man could live out his days up here, prospecting or hunting – fishing maybe, if you had a mind to do that". Aaron listened to him intently. "A shrewd man would easily make enough money to prosper. That was before the tourists moved in and the trails started to fill up and drive the wildlife fleeing into the forests," he said, sighing a little as he finished.

"Have you lived here alone?" Aaron asked. The old man chuckled at that, and continued "Company is not my thing, I prefer to look after myself, to listen to only me grumbling and complaining – that and the creatures out there in the trees," he said.

"I have known quite a few men who gave over their lives in the City to come up here though," he added. "One in particular – a man called William – spent the best part of forty years in these parts, living off the land, not interested in making a quick buck," he said, whilst seeming to stare off into the distance as if reminiscing.

"Did you know him well?" Aaron asked. "In a manner of speaking I guess I did," he replied with a smile. "Spent a fair amount of time together we did, chewing the fat and talking into the late hours as the sun went down". He bent and picked up an arm-sized length of wood, and threw it into the fire, sending up fresh sparks. "When he was younger – this William fella – he found himself on the wrong side of the local constable. Terrible business it was, a business that would be wise to run from – and so he had, right the way up here and out of sight of anyone but the animals and the occasional prospector".

Aaron listened as the old man continued to talk and lay the tale out to him, fascinated and eager enough to shuffle closer to him and the fire. "What was he in trouble for?"

"Oh it was over a woman – is it not always? William and another man who's name escapes me, got into a bar room quarrel over a girl called Sophia, who was arguably the most beautiful woman in town". He had a dreamy, almost faraway look in his eye as he continued, "Well, you know how it is, the drink taking effect and it was bound to happen – the other man was goading and belittling, so much so that William scooped up the bottle he was drinking from, and swung round handed at his head".

"Wow," Aaron said, "was he hurt?" The old man seemed to ponder this question for a moment, and then replied, "Well if you call stone dead hurt – then I guess that's just what he was".

"Man," Aaron whispered as he pictured the bottle connecting hard enough with the temple to take someone's life.

The old man continued. "Straight from the bar, he ran as if the hounds of hell themselves were chasing him, and he did not stop until he hit the first low slopes over there," he pointed back down the valley towards the lakes – the way that Aaron had come yesterday. "From what I recall, he found a small cave in the side of the mountain, and holed up for a week or two, only venturing out to find food – berries and other fruit that he could gather. The cave had a small fissure in the ceiling, from which trickled a steady flow of spring water – so he could stay there for as long as necessary".

"Did the authorities come looking for him?" Aaron asked.

"From time-to-time, he could here dogs and shouts as the search parties tried to battle their way through the thick terrain. They gave up though – after a few weeks – and took their search elsewhere, maybe thinking him dead or abroad".

"Finally, out he came, back into the land of the living and into the forests – that was his home thereafter".

"You could say he was a hermit of sorts, preferring to stay away from other people and keep his own counsel. The truth of it was – capture would mean certain prison and a lifetime of the same four walls, the same routine. That did not appeal to William – nor would it to any man

– and so this is the life he chose, out here in the open air with no one to answer to other than himself".

"What happened to him?" Aaron said.

"The cold got the better of him one year. It gets where your breath could freeze before it has left your lips when winter bites and takes hold - its icy grip seeming to never let up for months on end," he shuddered as if to emphasise the point. "Pneumonia it was in the end. Filled his lungs up with fluid right to the very top – there can't have been a spare inch of air left in them. He just packed in breathing and died in his bedroll".

They were both silent for a while, nothing passed between them other than the heat from the fire. Around them, the breeze caressed the branches of the trees, making them sway slightly as if slow dancing to the steady beat of a rhythm that only they could hear. Aaron let the words of the old man's story digest and flow over him as he sat quietly listening to the sounds of the night. "Well, it's getting late and I really should try and get some sleep – long day of hiking ahead of me in the morning" Aaron said and rose unsteadily to his feet, knees popping almost as loud as the fire.

"Maybe I will see you when the sun comes up, for breakfast?" He said, turning back to look at the old man. "Maybe you will," he replied. "I will be here – of that there can be no doubt".

Aaron made his way across the open ground to the trees that sheltered his tent. Pulling the zipper up and crawling inside, he thought of Wilf's face as he has said his goodbyes. Was there something odd about it? His brain registered a trickle of alarm deep down, but it was gone as quickly as it came and he lost it.

After the warmth of the fire, the sleeping bag was cool, but soon heated through as he settled in for the night. The breeze was slowing and losing strength, the trees no longer swaying, instead sighing – lulling him finally into a deep and dreamless sleep.

The heat of the early morning was hot and strong, turning the inside of the tent into an oven. Aaron woke slowly, coming round in stages until his was fully awake and thinking about breakfast. His stomach grumbled noisily as if it was prompting him to shift and prepare some food.

It was much cooler outside of the confines of the tent and the gentle breeze dried up the sweat on his body and made him shiver. It was going to be a glorious day – cloudless and hot. Birdsong rang out with an echo around the forest, sweet and melodious. He would eat breakfast and then break camp, heading off on the ever-rising climb towards the mountains – maybe hitting his target basecamp the day after.

Aaron stretched noisily, feeling his muscles and tendons creaking, as they too started to wake. He glanced through the trees towards the area where the fire had been last night but the dense foliage obscured most of the view, it was difficult to make anything out.

Fishing in his pack, he brought out a few pieces of dried jerky and a slice of bread – which was to be breakfast. Without bothering to dress, he made a path through the trees to see if the old man had awoken – which he suspected would be the case.

Emerging from the tree line, he could see nothing. Where the fire had been, a bare patch of earth with a few small rocks stood untouched, as if nothing had burned there for years – or ever for that matter.

Aaron was confused. He walked across and looked around the area where, only a few hours before, had been a roaring fire with a camp set out and an old man named

Wilf occupying the space that now contained a small spruce, with its roots beginning to stick out above ground.

Had he dreamed the whole thing? Was this the right spot? Quickly, he scanned the area in a 360-degree turn, checking behind the first line of trees in case he had misjudged the distance from the tent. Still nothing. Only the trees stared back, as if accusing and mocking him.

Retracing his steps, he walked backwards and forwards three times in slightly different directions and varying length – but still no sign. He decided to call out, "Wilf," "Wilf, are you here". The only sounds that greeted him were the echo and the sudden flap of wings as the birds close by decided to leave for quieter pastures.

Puzzled, he scoured the floor around the location of the fire - or where he thought it had been - looking for any sign of last night's activity – embers, discarded bits of food or indentations where they had been sitting. Still nothing.

Just as he was about to leave and give up the search – frustrated and questioning himself – something caught his eye next to a bush underneath one of the tallest trees. He had started to turn away, and he swung his head back with a snap. It was a flash of grey, just an instant and then gone, but it was enough to pique his interest.

A pile of stones stood next to a shrub of some sort, purple flowers standing proud against the almost completely green canvas of the forest around it. Bees and butterflies buzzed around – attracted by the blossom. The stones themselves - piled one on top of another, almost like a cairn - looked weathered and eroded from years of wind and rain battering them. A few of the stones had fallen off to one side, and lay discarded like broken teeth.

On closer inspection, it was clear that the monument had a human touch – the thick covering of moss and algae disguised much of it, but it was there nonetheless. A small plaque, hidden within the midst of the cairn, seemed to have writing on it. Aaron brushed a little of the debris away, revealing what looked to be an epitaph.

The letters had a worn, baleful look about them and it felt almost sacrilegious to be tampering with them – but still - he continued clearing away the dirt of ages until he revealed the writing beneath.

Five minutes passed. Aaron read the words, and then reread them – the bees continued to buzz around him, the butterflies continued to flutter in front of him, the birds continued to sing loudly above him. His mind went back to the previous night, the fire and the chatter, sharing a conversation with a man who had been dead for almost fifty years. He brain clamoured with the enormity of it.

The words on the stone read 'Here lies William Wilfred Parks, died June 22nd 1972'.

Much later, as Aaron trudged along the footpath that continued to wind its way closer and closer to the mountains ahead and above, his mind tried to make sense of it all. How could it be so? Who had buried him? Some of it made sense. The face – looking as though it belonged in a museum or a tomb in Egypt – its deep furrowed lines and dried out appearance made him curious at the time and now, even more so.

If all he had said was true – and Aaron had no reason to doubt it – then he would be able to trace him and find out some information when he returned to civilisation – whenever that would be.

The morning wore on, turning into the afternoon and beyond. The heat came with it – strong and oppressive – making every part of his body cry out for the cooling water of a stream or lake. How good it would feel to slip beneath the chilled surface and let the heat disappear from his clammy body. Throughout it all, his disbelieving mind clamoured with the thoughts of Wilf.

The path was becoming steeper to add to the discomfort and it was reaching the point whereby Aaron considered stopping and making camp more and more with each passing step. Around mid-afternoon, he finally did and dumped his pack to the ground, collapsing at the side of it and resting up. The heat of the sun beat relentlessly onto his exposed face, the skin baking and starting to burn on the bridge of the nose and around the eyes. He rolled over and began to make his camp.

The evening came cool and clear – the stars out in their multitudes and the moon bright, casting a ghostly glow across the forest floor. Aaron lay sleepless in his tent, thinking over the events of the previous night once more, playing them out in their entirety to try to find a chink or an explanation of some kind.

At midnight, he began to doze, fitfully at first, but then finally dropping off into a sleep where his dreams were vivid.

He dreamed he was walking through the forest at night, the ground hard and sharp beneath his feet – which were bare – as was the rest of his body. He was naked. On he walked, deeper into the trees, and away from the main path. Alarm rang its icy bell within his head but he paid no heed – just walking, moving further into the dark interior. A noise behind, a rustling, snapping sound – then a different noise, a growl? It sounded like a dog protecting a bone, only this one was not a dog – or at least not in the usual sense.

Aaron risked a look back over his shoulder. All he could see were trees. Turning back, he carried on walking, listening for the dog (thing) and casting the odd glance around.

When the sound came again, it was from directly in front – maybe two or three steps. He stood frozen, unable to move his feet. He looked down and they were stuck fast in mud, but the mud seemingly moved and swirled as if alive. The ankles disappeared, then the shins, calves, knees. He was sinking – quicksand – stuck solid. Out of the bushes in front of him stepped a dog. No, not a dog – a wolf. Fangs at least a foot long and dripping with saliva.

Its eyes were a blazing bright red, and fixed on his own. He could see death reflected in those eyes, it was coming for him, stepping slowly and covering the space between them. Aaron struggled but couldn't move, the quicksand had him in its maw, pulling him down and down. He tried to scream – mouth open wide but as he did, the sand flowed in and shut off any sound – choking and drowning. The wolf stepped over him and opened its great jaws wide, ready to clamp down.

Aaron woke and screamed out, battering the sides of tent as if trying to ward off the dream. Sweat ran from him in great rivers and the sleeping bag was soaked through. His heart was hammering inside of the chest cavity and the noise of it pounded loudly in his ears.

Slowly, he managed to get his breathing under control and the images from the dream began to fade, leaving only a disquieting feeling low down in his belly.

The night still had its hold over the world as Aaron peered out of the tent flap, the stars above bright and visible, although there was a faint dusting of dawn closing in from the East. He closed the tent back up and lay on the sleeping bag, the dream now almost forgotten.

The cry of an animal from the forest made him jump, and he realised how close to sleep he had been once more. Instead, his nerves fizzed a little and woke his senses. He could hear it walking by somewhere behind the tent, moving with stealth away from his camp. There was something else too. Another sound, a familiar sound, a little further off. It crackled – almost as if someone had a campfire burning.

Aaron scrambled to his knees and poked his head out into the night. The noise was unmistakable and clear. Looking to where it was coming from, he spotted it. The heartbeat that had slowed and steadied from his dream, now began to pick up pace once again, like a thoroughbred racing around the gallops. It was there, glowing bright and inviting.

A fire was crackling away no more than fifty yards from where he knelt, watching. Sitting facing him, the image distorted slightly behind the heat generated by the flames, was an old man. The man lifted his hand and waved.

THE EDGE OF

DAWN

Printed in Great Britain
by Amazon